LUCY and the ANVIL

A. KLINE

B TAYLOR

ADAM KLINE *and* **BRIAN TAYLOR**

for Sam Harrison Kline
and
for Noah Newton & Lily Pollard

Lucy and the Anvil

First Edition 2013

Text Copyright © 2013 by Adam Kline

Illustrations & Design Copyright © 2013 by Brian Taylor

Printed in the United States of America

Published by No Pity Press, Chicago & Dundee

ISBN: 978-0-9895538-0-3

www.nopitypress.com

ACKNOWLEDGEMENTS

The production of this book was made possible by the generosity
of precisely five hundred and sixty separate benefactors.
The following patrons bestowed gifts of exceptional note.

Melissa Aho	Emma, Leah & Tom Griffiths	Olivia Pichora
Malek Annabi	Kevin & Shannon Gruber	K. Michael Pollard
Mark Antholt	Ben Hafner	Sean Quinn
Anton & Nora	Luna Hartley	Team Reineke
Jack Auses	Amy Hartzler	The Reinekes
Scott R. Baker	The Heywood Family	Gail Riley
Maren & Hudson Bell	Lane Ikenberry	Roberto
Carson & Charlotte Binder	Carmen Italia	Ginny Ronayne
Brendan, Anne, Aidan & Dylan	Jagger, Jen & Neil Johnson	Rosenblatt
The Brice Family	Jo Johnson	Todd Rozycki
Sharon Buntin	Nathan 'neokinesis' Karklins	Greg Russell
Francisco Castanon	Keya Khayatian	Paul Russell
Cate & Jack	Crosby Vo Kirchner	Lisa Sallwasser
Luciana Cerdas	Rebecca Klein & Jeff Parfitt	Tom Scharpf
Connor Chase	J. Klenow	Chris Shepherd
Leslie E. Cook Jr.	Grandma & Grandpa Kline	Beth Siepmann
Jim Coudal	The Baron David Kowalski	Silver Skater
Sophie & Charlotte Cramp	Holly Kuzmich	Kevin Skoglund
Adam Dahlstedt & AddStudio	Mike Kuzmich	Izzy Slack
Audrey DeSchryver	David A. Lilly	Gerard Solis
Anne Duprey	Samantha Liskow	Keith Solomon
The FamiLee	Jason Maas	Spooky
Andrew Lee Feight	Mr. & Mrs. Charles S. Mauney	The Stambaugh Family
FiftyThree	Sean & Jen Murphy	Lee Stavroulis
Ashton Joshua Filies	Tommy Nagle	Linda Stevens
Alexander Fingerhut	Ashley Nath	Grandma & Grandpa Urso
H.E.R.A.L.D. Fingerhut	Grace Ann Newman	Walter & Elaine
Owen & Sophie Fingerhut	Jen & David Newton	Vaughn Wascovich
Mike Fish	Alan & Eileen Nicgorski	Wembly
Mark & Candace Fortuna	Ninja Baby	John & Kathleen Wilson
Chris Gallagher	OneSixthBruce	Scott Wren
Joseph B. Good	Viv & Mae Paulsen	T.K. Yamamoto
Grandpa Steve & Grandma Sharon	Neil Penick	Yvonne & Ethan
Wilder Green	Pete, Kerry, Olivia & Charlie	William & Mitchell Zumberge

and Mark Crisanti, whose anvil fell from the sky.

The anvil had never made a friend prior to Lucy.

He had been waiting a long time, but now the wait didn't seem so long.

Lucy had made the wait worthwhile.

So Lucy and the anvil set out to do the sorts of things that friends like to do. And the anvil decided to be the best friend in the history of friendship.

But the anvil wasn't very good at going to the park.

And he wasn't very good at going to the beach.

He wasn't good at sledding.

And he wasn't good at catch.

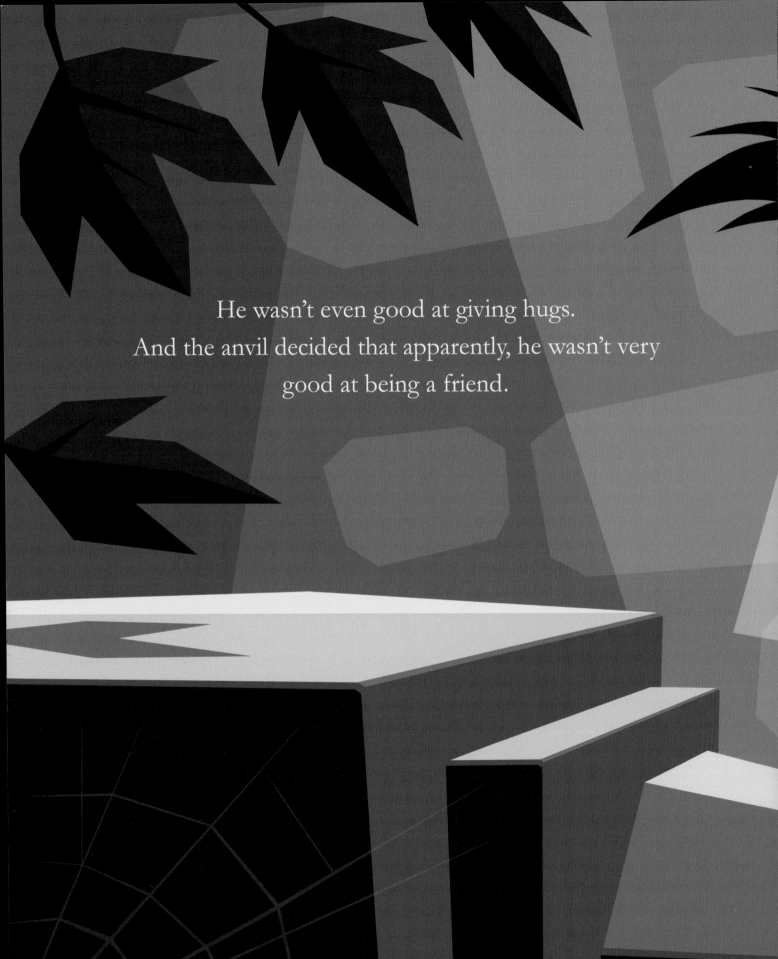

He wasn't even good at giving hugs.
And the anvil decided that apparently, he wasn't very
good at being a friend.

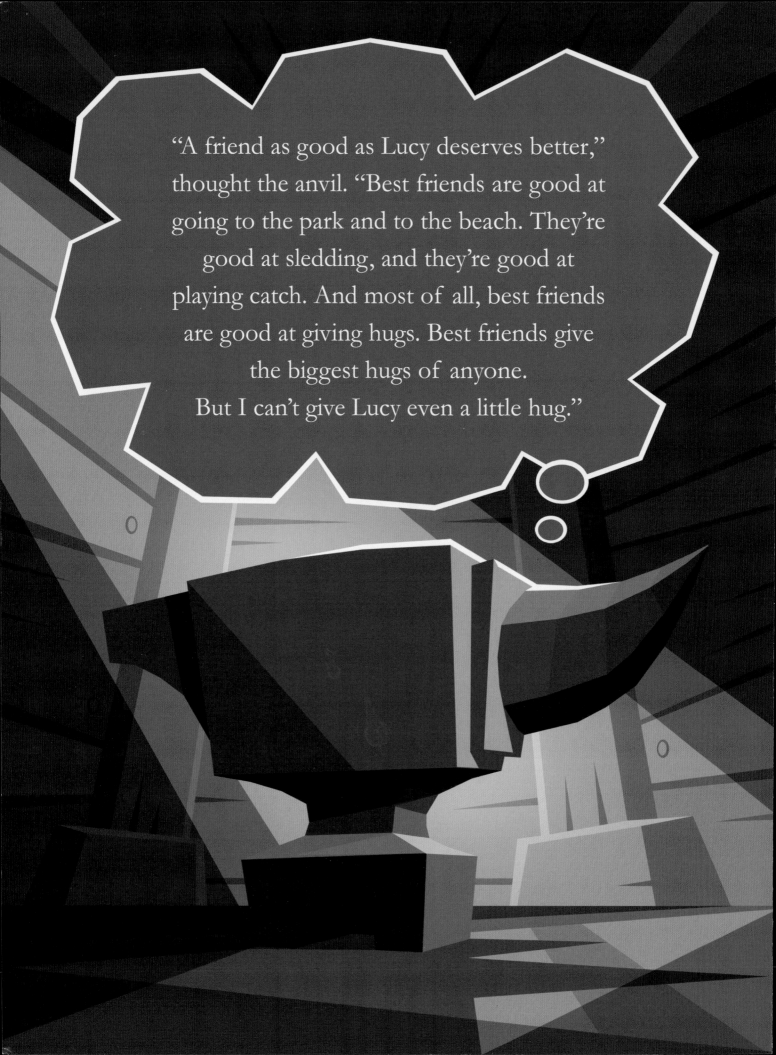

"A friend as good as Lucy deserves better," thought the anvil. "Best friends are good at going to the park and to the beach. They're good at sledding, and they're good at playing catch. And most of all, best friends are good at giving hugs. Best friends give the biggest hugs of anyone. But I can't give Lucy even a little hug."

So the anvil went and hid in the barn behind Lucy's house. And it was just like it had been before Lucy, except that instead of waiting for a friend to come along, the anvil mostly just thought about Lucy. Even in his dreams.

Then the storm came.
First there was rain.
Then there was thunder. And lightning, too.

And then came the wind.

It came across the park. And down the beach.
It took Lucy's sled. It took Lucy's ball.
And then the wind took Lucy's barn.

And the anvil suddenly realized that if he didn't
do something for his friend, the wind would
probably take Lucy, too.

Then the anvil saw her, through the storm.

He wasn't sure if Lucy had been crying, or if her face
was just wet from the rain. But it was Lucy, and that
was the important thing.

Lucy crawled toward the anvil, fighting against the wind.
The wind was terribly strong. But the anvil had faith in Lucy.

And when Lucy was very close, the anvil cried out,

"HUG ME!"

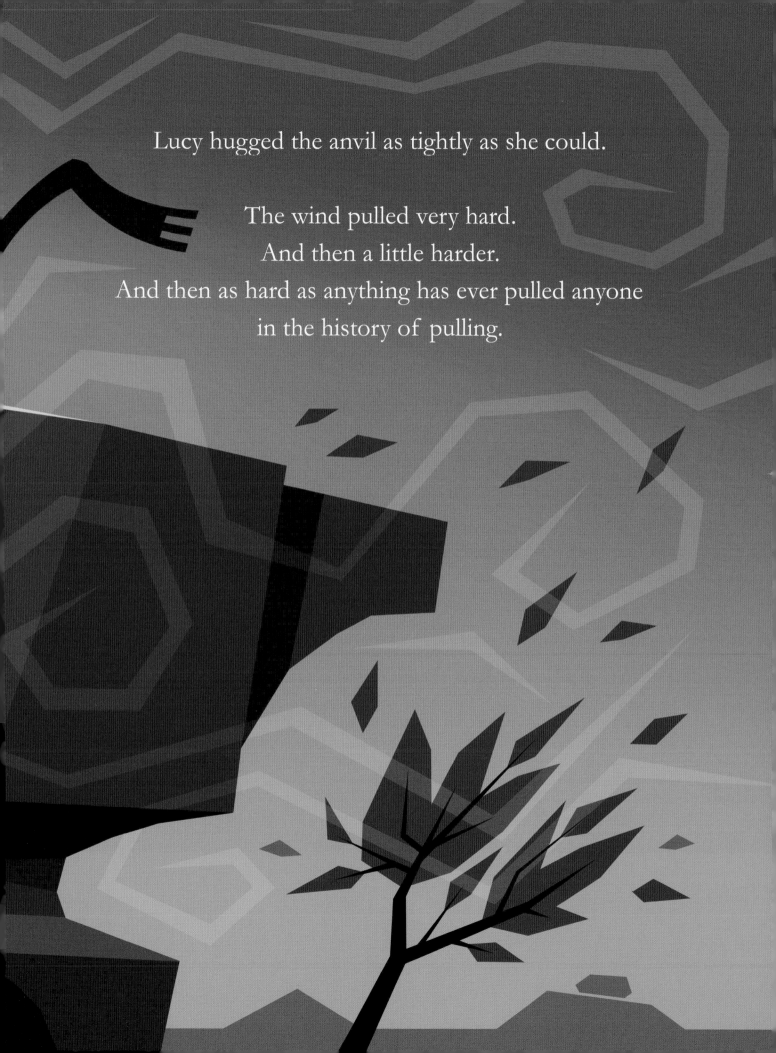

Lucy hugged the anvil as tightly as she could.

The wind pulled very hard.
And then a little harder.
And then as hard as anything has ever pulled anyone
in the history of pulling.

And finally, with one last howl of rage, the wind gave up.
Just like that.

But Lucy kept hugging the anvil,
just because she felt like it.

And the anvil realized that he was good at
something after all.

He wasn't good at giving hugs, but he was good at
getting them.

Adam Kline isn't very good at illustrating
children's books.

Brian Taylor isn't very good at writing them.

Maiba